Superhero Sam-Bam-Ka-Blam-Jam-Jimmy-Johnny-Jammy-Man

(another book with no pictures)

by Sam Evans

This is another book
with no pictures.

Are you ready to read another book with no pictures?

You know what happens when you read books with no pictures, *right?!*

Uh oh...

That's right.
More *super silly* words!

Oh no, you're not going to make me read another book full of super silly words, are you?

Hmmm… I wonder what this story is about.

Should we turn the page and find out?

KAZLAM!!!

Oh no! Superhero Sam-Bam-Ka-Blam-Jam-Jimmy-Johnny-Jammy-Man was under attack.

KAPOWZER!!!

But who could be attacking him?

KAGOOEY BLOOEY BOOGY WOOGY!!!

There could only be one person **evil** enough and **mean** enough to attack a Superhero.

Who could it be?

That's right. The evil

Dr. OCTOPO-
JACKALO-
HIPPOMO-
CROCOLO-
JECKEL
G.
BOB.

I've never heard of him.
Have you?

Well, Dr. OctopoJackaloHippomoCrockoloJeckel G. Bob was a mad scientist. He had invented lots of super silly weapons and now he was attacking the great city of

Kra*MAHN*alee
HOWzerknee
WHAPwhap
man**JO**bop.

Wait a minute… is that even a real city?

Dr. OctopoJackaloHippomoCrockoloJeckel G. Bob pulled out his

MANTARAY SUPERSPRAY BLASTAWAY LAZER-PHASER

He aimed it at Superhero Sam-Bam-Ka-Blam-Jam-Jimmy-Johnny-Jammy-Man.

And then he fired.

EEEEeeeeoooooooo waaaaaaaPOOOW zzzzziiiiinnnger!

Superhero Sam-Bam-Ka-Blam-Jam-Jimmy-Johnny-Jammy-Man jumped through the air.

SA-WOOOSH!

He looked radiant in his muscle-filled flannel pajama suit with his blankie-cape flying out behind him.

Flappa-wappa-flappa-wappa-flappa-wappa-slappa-slop.

Yes, his body was magnificent, but Superhero Sam-Bam-Ka-Blam-Jam-Jimmy-Johnny-Jammy-Man had one problem.

His voice sounded like a

teeny weeny little mouse.

Oh no! You mean I have to talk like a mouse, now?

"Why are you attacking the great city of

Kra*MAH*Nalee
HOWzerknee
WHAPwhap
man**JO**bop?"

he asked.

Dr. OctopoJackaloHippomoCrocoloJeckel G. Bob, on the other hand, sounded like **a fish.**

Under
WATER

Oh no...

"Because of the night lights," shouted
Dr. OctopoJackaloHippomoCrocoloJeckel G. Bob.

"I want all the
night lights
in the whole world!"

"All the **night lights**? But why?"

asked Superhero Sam-Bam-Ka-Blam-Jam-Jimmy-Johnny-Jammy-Man as he jumped on his Skyspy-o-ramajama-surfboard.

SKRIIIIIING

"Because of the **monsters** under the **beds**," Dr. OctopoJackaloHippomoCrocoloJeckel G. Bob cried.

"EEEEEEEEEEEEEEEEEEEEEEEEEEK!!!"
cried Superhero Sam-Bam-Ka-Blam-Jam-Jimmy-Johnny-Jammy-Man.

"Not the **monsters** under the **bed?!** Please don't hurt my *monsters*!"

"Oh, yes! It's always been about the **monsters**!

"Once I destroy all the night lights, the monsters will come out and destroy the world, and I will rule them all!" cried Dr. OctopoJackaloHippomoCrocoloJeckel G. Bob. as he loaded a gummy bear into his

yummy

gummy

bunny

gun!

He aimed and fired.

BLEGHMEL

LEMMELL

LEMMELL

LEGHM

Superhero Sam-Bam-Ka-Blam-Jam-Jimmy-Johnny-Jammy-Man gasped and raised his super deflect-a-field-o-shield-a-guard.

Ta-WAAAAAANG EEEEEEEEEEEE na-WOOOOOOP!

Then...

Dr. OctopoJackaloHippomoCrocoloJeckel G. Bob

let out the most evil
fish-under-water-laugh

the world has ever heard.

Oh no!
You mean I have to do an evil, under-the-water fish laugh?!

"Ah hah hah hah!! Eeee heeee heeee heee, oh ah, ha, ha, ha, heeee ho ho!"

Things were getting desperate. Superhero Sam-Bam-Ka-Blam-Jam-Jimmy-Johnny-Jammy-Man knew he needed to stop the Evil Dr. and he needed to do it soon.

There was only one option left - his greatest super power. He reached inside his suit, pulled out a music box and began to sing *the lullaby song...*

"Lullaby, sleep now,
your hero is here.

I will protect you
and calm all your fear.

Look at my muscles
I'm so super strong.

Don't worry
just look at me,
a-all night long."

Dr. OctopoJackaloHippomoCrocoloJeckel G. Bob, however, had come prepared - with noise-cancelling headphones, of course!

"Your song can't hurt me," he laughed.

"Besides, I know your superhero weakness."

"CHICKENS!!!"

He pulled a feathery white Leghorn Chicken out of his weapon bag and cuckooed his victory.

"Cluck, cluck, cluckety coo!"

Superhero Sam-Bam-Ka-Blam-Jam-Jimmy-Johnny-Jammy-Man went limp. His superhero powers were gone.

He was no match for chickens.

He looked around from the top of the building.

He saw the trees… the parking lot… the lake…

And then he had an idea.

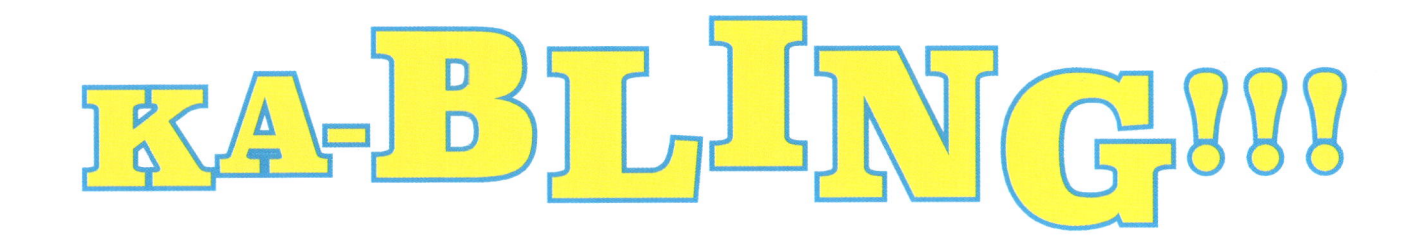

ka-BLING!!!

His superhero powers might be gone, but his brain and his body still worked. He ran towards the evil Dr. OctopoJackaloHippomoCrocoloJeckel G. Bob, grabbed him in a big bear hug, and kept running.

Then he jumped.

Right over the edge of the building.

AAAAIIIIEEEEEeeee aaaaaaoOOOoooooo-IaaaAAA wooooOmaAAAaa-neeeEEee uuuUUUuuhhh-hooooOaaaaoo oooooWWWW-AaaahrrrreeeeEE!!!

KERSPLAAAAAASH!!!

They had landed right in the lake.

Dr. OctopoJackaloHippomoCrocoloJeckel G. Bob flailed about in the water.

"Help! I can't swim"

Superhero Sam-Bam-Ka-Blam-Jam-Jimmy-Johnny-Jammy-Man grabbed the Evil Dr. and pulled him to the shore where the police were waiting.

"Good job, Superhero Sam-Bam-Ka-Blam-Jam-Jimmy-Johnny-Jammy-Man," they said.

"Never fear, good citizens of **Kra*MAH*Nalee HOWzerkneeWHAPwhapmanJObop**.

Whenever villains like

Dr. OctopoJackaloHippomoCrocoloJeckel G. Bob

are near, just call for

Superhero Sam-Bam-Ka-Blam-Jam-Jimmy-Johnny-Jammy-Man

and I'll…"

"Cluck, Cluck, Cuckoo!"
called out the Leghorn chicken.

"Shoo!"

yelled Superhero Sam-Bam-Ka-Blam-Jam-Jimmy-Johnny-Jammy-Man.

"Leave me alone.

"Stop following me!"

But the chicken wouldn't leave him alone. In fact, it followed him all the way home and into his apartment. Superhero Sam-Bam-Ka-Blam-Jam-Jimmy-Johnny-Jammy-Man was just too tired to care.

"Goodnight, little chicken,"

he said.

Then he turned out his **night light.**

"Cluck, Cluck, Cu..."

CHOMP!

"Good monster."

the end.

Printed in Great Britain
by Amazon